The
Summer House
Cat

The Summer House Cat

by Michele Granger
illustrated by Lindy Strauss

E. P. DUTTON · NEW YORK

Library of Congress Cataloging-in-Publication Data

Granger, Michele.
    The summer house cat.

    Summary: A family on vacation cares for a little
yellow cat, which the children long to take home with
them when they leave.
    [1. Cats—Fiction] I. Strauss, Lindy, ill. II. Title.
PZ7.G76619 1989 [Fic] 88-31000
ISBN 0-525-44488-2

Published in the United States by E. P. Dutton,
a division of Penguin Books USA Inc.

Published simultaneously in Canada by
Fitzhenry & Whiteside Limited, Toronto

Printed in the U.S.A.   First Edition
10 9 8 7 6 5 4 3 2 1

for Courtney, with love
M.G.

for Oak Bluffs, Massachusetts,
the town that writes
its name in petunias
L.S.

Contents

· 1 ·

A Note from a Visitor

Charlotte saw the note about the cat as soon as they got to the summer house. It was stuck on the refrigerator door with an old Chiquita banana sticker that was curling up around the edges but still had some sticky left in the middle. It said:

To whom it may concern,
The little yellow cat is very sweet. She is also very hungry. There is a bag of cat food under the kitchen counter. If you have it in your heart to feed her, I believe you will be doing an act of kindness.

A Visitor

Charlotte yanked the note down.

"Mom, Daddy," she yelled, banging out the screen door. "Look at this. There's a cat here somewhere."

Mom stood on the front porch with her arms spread wide.

"Isn't it just lovely, Charlotte?"

"What?"

"The house. The yard. The whole island," said Mom. "And to think we got this from a description over the phone last January."

"You're not listening," said Charlotte. "There's a cat here. Look." Charlotte held the note so that Mom could read it. "Do you think we can find her?" asked Charlotte.

"I don't know," said Mom. "We can try."

Daddy came up the porch steps with his arms loaded down.

"How about giving me a hand here?" he said.

"I have to find a cat first," Charlotte said, running off. "Leave my stuff. I'll get it after."

"I coming too," said Tessa. Charlotte's little sister dropped her basket of toys on the grass and followed.

"After *what*?" Daddy yelled.

But Charlotte kept running.

"Kitty, kitty, kitty," she called in a very high voice, racing around the yard.

"Kitty, kitty, kitty," called Tessa. Tessa copied her all the time.

They ran down the hill in front of the summer house to the old stone wall at the edge of the yard, calling and calling.

Then they went around behind the house

to look. There was a long clothesline
stretched across the yard. The poles that held
it up looked old and splintery. Three faded
towels waved at them from the line.

The visitor must have left those out here,
thought Charlotte. But there was no cat in
the backyard either.

"Kitty, kitty, kitty." They called and
called, but the cat didn't come.

"Look, Tessa," Charlotte said. "There's a
deck up over the front porch. Lct's go look
from there."

Tessa pointed. "No steps," she said.

"There must be a way to get out there from inside the house," said Charlotte. "C'mon."

The screen door banged behind them as Charlotte and Tessa ran back inside.

"Mom," Charlotte called, running up the stairs to the second floor, "how do you get out to the deck?"

Mom came out of the bedroom with a stack of clothes draped over her arm.

"That door there," she said, pointing across the hall.

Charlotte tried to open the door, but it was stuck. She threw her weight against it— "Uh!"—and the door swung out. Charlotte stepped over the threshold with Tessa behind her.

"Wow." Charlotte looked around her. "You can see the whole world from up here, Tessa."

"Boats!" said Tessa. "I see 'em."

"That's the ocean," said Charlotte. "Hey, Mom, you can see the ocean from up here."

"I know," Mom called back. "Beautiful!"

"But I don't see a cat, Tessa. Do you?" Charlotte asked.

"No kitty," said Tessa.

Charlotte went back inside.

"Where's my room, Mom?"

"Yours *and* Tessa's," said Mom. "Right here. Isn't it nice? So big and bright."

"This is my bed." Charlotte bounced on the bed by the window.

"*My* bed." Tessa said, bouncing next to her.

"*That* one's yours, Tessa," said Charlotte. She pointed to the one across the room. "We each have our own bed."

"Oh." Tessa sat down on the other one. "*My* bed," she said.

"And keep all your stuff over on *that* side, Tessa," said Charlotte. "I'd better not find *one* thing of yours over here."

Mom came in. "This room's plenty big enough for both of you," she said. "Lots of room for all your possessions, Charlotte."

"Which are still on the front porch, by the way," Daddy said, joining them.

"OK, I'll get them," said Charlotte. "But can I at least eat something first? I'm starving."

"I starving, too," said Tessa.

"Those sandwiches we brought are downstairs in the cooler," Daddy said. "But I'd better see you unpacking as soon as you finish your last bite."

Half-filled cartons and bags covered the kitchen floor and countertop, and the cabinet doors hung open.

"Step carefully," Daddy warned. "It's taking me a while to get organized here."

"No kidding," said Charlotte.

"Eureka!" Daddy held up two sandwiches in little plastic bags. "All the way from New Jersey and not a scratch on 'em."

He handed one to Charlotte and one to Tessa.

"And for your luncheon beverage, the very fincst apple juice."

Daddy popped the tabs on two small cans of juice and gave one to each of them.

"We can't find the cat in the note," Charlotte said, her mouth full of sandwich. "We looked everywhere."

"What note?" asked Daddy.

"Here. Look." Charlotte dug the paper from her shorts pocket.

"Hmmm," said Daddy, reading. "Nope. Haven't seen him."

"*Her,*" said Charlotte. "The note says *she.*"

"Whoever," said Daddy. "There's no cat food here, either. So maybe it's just as well. It must be an old note."

Mom came into the kitchen.

"Have you come across my sandwich yet?" she asked. "Suddenly I'm ravenous."

"It's in the cooler somewhere," Daddy said.

"The cat might come later, though," said Charlotte. "We have to get some food for her."

"She might," agreed Mom. "Aha! Here it

is!" She unwrapped her sandwich and took a bite.

"How about it, Charlotte?" said Daddy. "Your stuff on the porch, remember?"

"Yeah, yeah," Charlotte said. "I'm going. I just hope the cat comes, that's all."

"I hope her comes, too," said Tessa. She followed Charlotte out.

Charlotte got as far as pushing her things together in a pile, then she sank onto the porch floor and hugged her knees.

"I bet Mom hopes the cat comes, too," she said to Tessa. "She really likes cats. She even likes Howard."

"Howard bite me," Tessa said, rubbing the back of her hand.

"Yeah, and he scratches too," Charlotte said. "He bites and scratches everyone but Mom."

Howard was their cat at home in New Jersey. He was big and orange and fluffy, a beautiful cat, but unpredictable. Nora from down the street was taking care of him while they were away. Nora didn't seem afraid of Howard, but she was almost thirteen and wasn't afraid of much of anything.

Later they made a trip to the Island Grocery Store.

Mom thought that it was silly to buy cat food when they hadn't even seen a cat yet.

But Charlotte convinced her that they could bring the food home to Howard if it didn't get eaten.

"Only get Meow Mix," said Mom. "You know how finicky Howard is about his food." Charlotte went off to look and came back hugging a big yellow bag.

"Meow Mix, Howard's favorite," she said, tossing the cat food into the grocery cart.

"Let's cross our fingers, Tessa," Charlotte said when they were in the car, heading back to the summer house. "If we close our eyes and cross our fingers all the way back, the cat will be there."

Charlotte crossed her fingers on both hands and squeezed her eyes shut tight.

"Are your eyes shut, Tessa?" Charlotte asked.

"Yes."

"Are your fingers crossed?"

"Yes. It hurts me," said Tessa.

"Don't uncross them. We're almost there. And don't open your eyes till Mom stops the car."

"This kind of thing doesn't always work," Mom said.

"Well, it might," said Charlotte.

Mom turned off the car.

"OK. Open your eyes!" Charlotte shouted to Tessa.

She did. Charlotte did, too. No cat. No cat anywhere.

"I thought you'd never get back," Daddy called from the deck. He was up there with his feet on the rail, reading a book. "Get your suits on and we'll go down to the beach. That's what we came for."

It was late afternoon by the time they got to the beach.

The wind was blowing and the sunlight was weakening, but Charlotte threw her sweat shirt onto the sand and ran straight into the water. Tessa went after her, but she jumped back squealing when the ocean foam rushed up at her, and ran to Mom.

Daddy dove into an incoming wave.

"Ho-o-o!" he said, shaking water from his hair. "Brisk!"

"I'm staying right here with Tessa today," Mom said. She pulled up the hood of her sweat shirt and yanked the strings till her face just peeked out, looking very small.

Charlotte only got wet once. The water was a little cold, even for her. Mostly she practiced doing cartwheels. Tessa practiced doing somersaults, but she called them cartwheels. Her hair was full of sand.

They stayed at the beach until the sky started turning pink and almost everyone else had gone home.

In the car on the way back to the summer house, Charlotte and Tessa crossed their fingers again, both hands, and squeezed their eyes shut tight.

Charlotte said it was important to keep them shut *very* tight. "Just because it didn't work last time doesn't mean it's not going to work this time," she said.

"We're almost there," Charlotte shouted as they bumped up the long dirt-and-rock driveway to the house. Finally, the car stopped.

"OK!" yelled Charlotte. They uncrossed their fingers. They opened their eyes. And there she was.

A little yellow cat ran up to the car as if she had been waiting for them the whole time.

"It's her!" Charlotte shrieked. "I know it's her."

2

Exploring

The little yellow cat followed them up onto the porch and rubbed back and forth across Mom's ankles as she turned the key in the lock at the back door.

"Mom, hurry up," said Charlotte. "Can't you see that the cat is starving?"

"She certainly looks hungry," Mom said.

She did. Charlotte could see her ribs sticking out under her fur. She wasn't really yellow, though. She was more of a pinky beige color. But Charlotte knew it was the little yellow cat in the note.

"Remember, this is a 'No Pets' house," Daddy said. "The cat will have to stay outside."

Charlotte glared at him, but she pushed the cat back gently with the toe of her sneaker when Mom opened the door.

Charlotte scooped out some Meow Mix and clattered it into a big metal bowl. Then she filled a smaller bowl halfway with water.

"Here I come, little cat!" Charlotte called. "Don't you worry. I'm here to take care of you now."

"I do it!" Tessa yelled, trying to pull the bowl out of Charlotte's hands.

"Here, take it," Charlotte said, shoving the bowl at her. "I'll bring the water. I know you'll spill it if you bring it."

The cat reached up and tried to push her face into the bowl as Tessa put it down on the porch floor.

"Her's biting me," Tessa squeaked, nearly dropping the bowl.

"Oh, she is *not*, Tessa," Charlotte said. "She's not like Howard. This is a sweet little cat that we can feed all by ourselves."

"Howard bite me," said Tessa.

"And here's your water," Charlotte said

grandly as she set it down next to the Meow Mix.

The cat paid no attention to Charlotte or the bowl of water. She wanted food. She ate and ate until the Meow Mix was all gone. Then she sniffed at the empty bowl and looked up at Charlotte expectantly.

"She's still hungry," Charlotte said, jumping up. "*I'll* get the food this time."

"No fair!" Tessa yelled. But Charlotte grabbed the bowl and ran inside before Tessa could stop her.

"We got here just in time," Charlotte yelled up the stairs. "This little cat really needs me to take care of her."

"Don't get any ideas, Charlotte," Daddy hollered back. "We're *not* keeping this cat."

Charlotte didn't answer, but ran back outside with the bowl of cat food.

The cat ate only a little bit out of the second bowl. Then she stopped and walked away from it, holding her tail high in the air.

Charlotte reached down and stroked her gently from her head, down her bony back, and up to the soft tip of her tail. The cat pushed herself into Charlotte's hand as she did it. She didn't run away.

What a wonderful cat, thought Charlotte. Not like Howard at all.

"You can pet her, Tessa," Charlotte whispered. "She doesn't bite."

"I don't want to," Tessa answered, looking

down at her fingers as she twisted them together over her tummy.

"OK, then maybe you will tomorrow,
Tessa. Or the next day or the day after
that." Charlotte grabbed the cat up in a hug.
" 'Cause you're going to stay with us now,
aren't you, little cat?"

The next morning, Charlotte was the first
one awake. "Tessa, wake up," she whispered, shaking her just a bit. "Let's find the
cat."

"My turn," said Tessa, pulling her legs out
from under the tangle of sheets. "I feed
her."

They ran downstairs. Charlotte pulled the
door open. The cat was sitting on the porch,
waiting for them to pour more Meow Mix into her bowl and fill her dish with water.

"See? I don't spill it," Tessa bragged, setting her bowl down next to Charlotte's.

"Big deal, Tessa," said Charlotte. "It's only half full. When *I* was three, I used to carry great big bowls full of water all the time."

"Oh," said Tessa.

Charlotte slid down onto her stomach and lay on the porch floor. The warmth from the floorboards seeped up through the thin cloth of her summer nightgown.

Tessa sat beside her, in pajamas with tiny blue flowers all over them, her legs folded up Indian style. They watched the cat eat.

"You don't belong to anyone. Do you, little yellow cat?" Charlotte asked her. "Well, don't worry. I'll take care of you."

Charlotte trailed her hand lightly down the cat's back. Then suddenly she jumped up. "Let's go exploring, Tessa," she said. "C'mon. It's fun." Charlotte started running down the hill toward the stone wall at the edge of the yard.

"I got jammies," said Tessa.

"It's OK to go like this," Charlotte said, lifting her nightgown hem. "We're on vacation."

Tessa followed Charlotte. So did the cat. The grass felt all scrubby and rough under Charlotte's bare feet.

"Look, Tessa," Charlotte said, "there's a hole in the wall, like the kind chipmunks live in."

The cat poked her nose into the hole as if she were checking for them. Nothing came out.

"Maybe they're asleep," Charlotte said.

"Chimpmucks sleeping," said Tessa.

They waited and watched the hole. After a while, Charlotte said, "C'mon, Tessa. This is boring. The chipmunks are staying inside today. Let's go over where those prickly bushes are." She ran in that direction before Tessa could answer. Tessa and the cat ran after her.

"Blackberries!" Charlotte shouted. "Let's pick them!"

"I can eat them?" Tessa asked.

"Oh, yes. They're very good to eat," Charlotte said, as if she really knew.

"Yuck!" Tessa spit her blackberry out onto the grass. Purply black juice dribbled down her chin and onto the front of her pajamas. "I don't like it."

Charlotte swallowed hers, but Tessa was right. It *was* yucky.

"Grown-ups like these, I think," Charlotte said. "Or maybe cats."

Charlotte squatted down and held a blackberry out to the cat. She sniffed at it. Then her tiny pink tongue flicked out to lick at Charlotte's hand. She licked all around the blackberry without touching it. Charlotte pulled her hand back a bit. The cat's tongue felt scratchy. Charlotte had never gotten close enough for Howard to lick her hand. She wouldn't have dared.

"She's licking me, Tessa," Charlotte said, feeling brave. "Put your hand down here. See if she'll lick you too."

"No!" said Tessa. "Don't want to."

"Oh, don't be such a baby, Tessa. It doesn't hurt. She's a sweet cat." Charlotte jumped up. "But she doesn't like blackberries either. Let's go around back." Charlotte threw what was left of her berries onto the grass and wiped her hands on her nightgown as she ran.

She was standing by a clump of tall grass and wildflowers in the backyard when Tessa and the cat came around the corner of the summer house.

"Blowies!" cried Tessa.

"Those are just dandelion puffs, Tessa," said Charlotte. "But look at these."

Charlotte reached for a tall pink flower, pushing some of the grass aside with her arms. "Oh, look what's in here, Tessa. A little wagon!"

"*My* wagon," said Tessa.

"It's the summer house's wagon," Charlotte said, dragging it out onto the grass. "But we can use it while we're here."

"They forgot all about this wagon," Charlotte said, rubbing at its side with her finger. "It's gotten all rusty and old out here."

"*My* wagon," Tessa said, pulling at its handle.

"Let's give the cat a ride," Charlotte said. "I'll put her in and you pull the wagon." Tessa looked like she didn't want to, but she didn't say no.

Charlotte gently lifted the cat into the wagon. "OK, Tessa, get moving before she jumps out."

Tessa carefully picked up the wagon handle, watching the cat as she did it.

"Go on, Tessa," Charlotte said. "Pull it."

Tessa gripped the handle with both hands and tugged. The wheels were frozen with rust and wouldn't turn. Then suddenly the wagon lurched forward, and the cat sprang away and vanished into the high, pale grass.

"Look what you did, Tessa," said Charlotte. "You scared her off."

"I didn't mean to," said Tessa. She looked around hopelessly, her eyes suddenly shiny with tears. "I find kitty."

"Forget it, Tessa," said Charlotte. "We'll find her later. It's OK."

"OK?" Tessa asked.

"Yeah," Charlotte said. "You get in and I'll pull you back to the house."

Tessa climbed into the wagon. She rubbed at her wet cheeks with rust-stained palms, leaving orange streaks.

"*My* wagon," she said, patting its sides.

"All right. It's *your* wagon, but it's *my* cat you scared off," Charlotte said.

The wagon bumped along over the grass. Its wheels turned sluggishly, as if they had just been woken from a long nap.

"*My* cat," said Tessa.

"All right, all right, *our* cat," said Charlotte. "She's *our* cat, then, Tessa. You know, Daddy said not to get any ideas about her.

But I already have lots of ideas about that little yellow cat and me."

"Me too," said Tessa. "Me too."

3

A Day at the Beach

For the fourth morning in a row, the cat was waiting for Charlotte when she came out onto the porch. Charlotte brought out a bowl of food and some fresh water and sat down on the step to watch her eat. When the cat had taken her last bite of Meow Mix, she looked up at Charlotte.

"I'll see you as soon as I get back from the beach," Charlotte told her.

"C'mon, Charlotte," Daddy called from the car. "We want to get going."

Charlotte kissed the top of the little cat's head and slowly walked to the car.

"I don't see why we have to go so early,"

Charlotte said, clicking her seat belt together. "I want to stay with my cat."

"*Your* cat?" said Daddy. He backed the station wagon down the long, bumpy driveway. "She's the summer house's cat, Charlotte. And don't you forget it." He turned left onto the road.

"Oh, c'mon, you two," said Mom. "It's too nice a day to argue. And we'll have the whole day at the beach today. We don't have to rush back for anything."

"The *whole* day," said Charlotte. "Sounds boring. Then I'll hardly get to see my cat at all."

Charlotte waited for Daddy to say something else, but he didn't.

"She'll be there when we get back," said Mom. "And I suggest you improve your attitude, my dear, or you can wait in the car until you do."

"Charlotte's not coming?" said Tessa.

"I hope she is," said Mom.

"Look at that," said Daddy. He pulled

into the beach parking lot. "It looks like we're the first ones here."

"No one else is crazy enough to come out this early," said Charlotte.

"Charlotte." Mom shot her a warning look.

"OK, OK," Charlotte said, climbing out. "See? I'm smiling. I'm having a wonderful time."

"Charlotte's coming!" said Tessa. She grabbed Charlotte's hand and pulled her along the path to the beach. "Make a castle with me," she said.

"All right, Tessa." Charlotte dropped her beach bag on the sand and went down to the water, swinging a plastic bucket. She scooped watery sand into the bucket and carried it back to their blanket.

"Make a castle," whined Tessa.

"I *am*," said Charlotte. "This is how you do it."

She lifted a handful of mud from the bucket and let it trickle through her fingers onto the sand.

"See, Tessa," said Charlotte. "We're making a castle out of dribbles. You just keep dribbling mud on top, and it all piles up to make a castle."

Tessa looked doubtful, but she dropped her handful of mud onto Charlotte's.

"That's it," said Charlotte, even though Tessa's was more of a splat than a dribble. "Now, do another one."

Dribble. Dribble. Dribble. Splat!

"Tessa, you get the water this time." Charlotte thrust the bucket at her.

"Don't want to," said Tessa. "Bean fish." She pointed at the water.

"Bean fish!" said Charlotte. "There's no such thing."

"Uh-huh," Tessa said. "I see jelly bean fish on the sand."

"You are so dumb." Charlotte grabbed the bucket and headed for the water. She could hear Mom and Daddy laughing behind her.

They were all waiting by the dribble castle when Charlotte got back.

"Want some help?" said Mom.

"Yeah," said Charlotte. "Now it's really going to get big, Tessa. Wait'll you see."

Dribble. Blop! Dribble.

Charlotte scooped more mud from the bucket. "I wonder what the little cat does all day while we're gone?" she said.

"Chases grasshoppers and takes naps in the sun," said Daddy.

"Dreams of field mice," said Mom.

"She dreams about me," said Charlotte. "She misses me when I'm not there."

"I doubt it," said Daddy. "That cat's used to being alone."

"She does so dream about me," said Charlotte, dripping wet sand. "She loves me."

"OK, OK," said Daddy. "She loves you."

"Kitty loves *me*." Tessa's handful of mud splattered on top.

"That's great," said Daddy. "But just remember that it's a love 'em and leave 'em situation we've got here."

"What a way to put it," said Mom.

"I'm only being honest," Daddy said.

Charlotte jumped up. "I'm going in the water." She stomped down the beach.

"What about your castle?" asked Mom.

"Finish it without me," said Charlotte.

Charlotte walked into the ocean and didn't turn back to look at them. She waded out till she was up to her waist, then lay back in the water to float. Cold water crept into her ears, taking away the sounds of the outside.

No one loves the cat like I do, she thought. Not even Tessa.

A wave rocked her, and Charlotte held her breath to keep out a ripple that washed over her face. She floated for what seemed like a long time. Then she rolled over and began to swim. She was used to swimming in the town pool at home. Here, there was no black line on the bottom to keep her going straight. And after only a few strokes, her fingers raked the sand. When she stood, the water only came up to her knees.

How did I get so close in? she wondered. I want to be out, way far out, and not near *them.*

She saw the ferry on its way back to Point Judith, moving along the line where the sky met the water. She swam that way and kept swimming and swimming.

Suddenly, from the side, Charlotte saw a big dark shape coming toward her. A shark!

Her heart jumped. She bolted upright, treading water. But it wasn't a shark. It was a dog, a big black dog with a yellow tennis ball in his mouth. And near the dog was a girl, bobbing in the water.

"That's Max. He won't hurt you," the girl said, laughing.

"What's he doing out here, so far?" asked Charlotte. "He scared me."

"Sorry," said the girl. "He's a Labrador. He loves the water."

"Oh. I'm Charlotte," Charlotte said, not knowing what else to say.

"I'm Emily," said the girl. Then she ducked under a wave and began to swim toward the beach, with Max paddling after her. Charlotte followed them as if she'd meant to go that way, too.

Finally, someone *my* age, thought Charlotte.

When they got to shore, Max got all excited, barking and nosing his tennis ball along the sand.

"Throw it for him. Out into the water," said Emily.

Charlotte picked up the soggy, sandy ball and threw it as far as she could. Max went right after it, with the waves breaking over him as he swam. Then he headed back in with the tennis ball in his mouth.

"He got it!" Charlotte shouted.

"He always does," said Emily. "No matter how big the waves are. Do you have a dog?"

"No," said Charlotte. "We have a cat named Howard. But he's not friendly, like Max. He bites and scratches. I hate him, and my little sister's really scared of him."

"That's awful," said Emily.

"Yeah," said Charlotte. "But I'm taking care of a wonderful cat here."

"For someone else, you mean?" asked Emily.

"Well, not exactly," said Charlotte. "I don't think anyone actually owns her."

"Then you can have her," said Emily.

"I wish," said Charlotte. "Are you here on vacation?"

"Just for today," said Emily. "Tomorrow we go to Newport. Get down, Max."

"Then you're staying over?" asked Charlotte.

"Yeah," said Emily. "We sleep on my dad's boat."

"Max came with you on a boat?" Charlotte asked.

"All the way from New York City," said Emily, throwing Max's ball down the beach. "That's where my dad lives."

"Where's your mom?" asked Charlotte.

"She's home in Massachusetts," said Emily. "They're divorced. I stay with my dad in the summer."

"Don't you miss him when you're in Massachusetts?" asked Charlotte.

"Yeah," said Emily. "And sometimes I miss my mom in the summer. What grade are you going into?"

"Third," said Charlotte.

"Me too," said Emily. "Want to take Max for a walk?"

"Sure," said Charlotte.

"Dad!" Emily hollered. "We're taking Max for a walk."

A man in a tennis hat and sunglasses saluted them from his beach chair.

He looks so nice, thought Charlotte. I wonder why they got a divorce?

Max ran ahead of them but kept coming back to nudge their legs with his sandy nose.

"Go on, Max." Emily gently pushed him away. "Are you here on vacation?"

"For a week," said Charlotte. "We rented a summer house."

"Who's with you?" asked Emily.

"Oh, my mom and my dad and my little sister, Tessa."

"Charlotte!" Mom waved from her beach chair. "Here we are!"

"My mom," Charlotte said, rolling her eyes. "And my baby sister, a real pain."

"C'mon, Emily," said Charlotte. "I'd better tell them where I'm going."

"I'll wait here," said Emily. "Max jumps all over people." Emily threw Max's ball out into the water.

"OK." Charlotte ran up to Mom and Daddy, who was dozing under his straw hat.

"Who's your new friend?" asked Mom.

"Emily," said Charlotte. "And Max, her dog. I met them out swimming."

"So I saw," said Mom. "Don't worry. We've been watching you the whole time."

"Yeah. Daddy's really watching," said Charlotte.

"He just went to sleep a minute ago," said Mom. "Let up on your father, why don't you, Charlotte?"

"But he keeps saying mean things about my cat," said Charlotte.

"I think you're being a bit sensitive," said Mom.

"Well, anyway, we're taking Max for a walk," said Charlotte. "Can you keep Tessa here? I don't want her tagging along with us."

"Go on," said Mom. "She'd probably be afraid of the dog anyway."

"See you," Charlotte said, and ran back to Emily and Max.

"Let's go before Tessa follows us," she said. But when she looked, Tessa was sitting in the sand next to Mom's chair, drinking a can of juice.

Emily and Charlotte walked and walked, stopping every so often to throw Max's ball for him. When Charlotte looked back, she couldn't see Mom or Dad or Tessa anymore. They were lost in a clutter of other people's beach chairs and striped umbrellas.

"Too bad you can't stay longer," said Charlotte. "We're here till Sunday, and I don't have anyone I can really play with. You know, my own age."

"Me, either," said Emily. "But at least you have a little sister."

"Well, you have Max, and you get to sleep on a boat."

"I still wish I had a sister," said Emily.

They walked for a while without talking. The tide was going out, leaving the sand flat and hard. It glinted here and there, as if it held the tiniest of twinkling Christmas lights.

"We'd better head back," Emily said. "My dad said we couldn't stay here too long. He wants to have lunch in town. He knows a good place to go."

"What will you do with Max?" asked Charlotte.

"Oh, he'll be OK in the cabin of the boat," said Emily. "He knows we always come back for him."

"That's good," said Charlotte. "It's awful when people just leave animals all alone. Max is lucky to have you and your dad."

Too bad your mom's not here, too, thought Charlotte.

"Did you hear that, Max?" Emily bent down to hold Max's muzzle in her hands. Max dropped his ball and licked Emily's face. "Charlotte says you're a lucky, lucky boy."

"Too bad my little cat isn't lucky like Max," said Charlotte.

4

Charlotte Tells Mom

Charlotte sat on the wooden bench that went all around the edge of the deck. She held a tortilla chip out for the cat, who nibbled at it with small, delicate bites.

"I wish you could have met Emily," she said to the cat. "She would have loved you, too."

"Her likes it," Tessa said, plunking down on the bench. She held another chip out to the cat. "Here, kitty."

"Tessa, let her finish this one, will you?" said Charlotte. "You're always butting in."

Tessa shrugged and took a bite of the chip. Daddy came out.

"How did that cat get up here?" he asked.

"You know she's not allowed inside the house."

"We didn't bring her in the house," said Charlotte. "She climbed up the wall of the outside shower stall and jumped from the roof down here to the bench."

"Oh." Daddy slouched into a canvas chair and looked off at the sailboats.

The little cat turned around and settled into a furry circle on Charlotte's lap.

"Pretty smart, huh?" Charlotte asked.

"Brilliant," said Daddy, "for an animal with a brain the size of a marble."

"I'll bet Emily's father doesn't say mean things about animals," said Charlotte. "He even takes his dog with them on his boat."

"Sounds like a regular prince," said Daddy.

"Who does?" Mom came out and sat in the other canvas chair.

"Daddy's making fun of Emily's father just because he really loves animals and Daddy doesn't."

"That's not what's going on at all," said

Daddy. "Have I ever been mean to Howard?"

"Howard," groaned Charlotte.

"Howard . . . " began Tessa.

"Tessa, don't say it. I know. Howard bit you. Everyone in the world knows about it."

"Him scratch me, too."

"*This* cat doesn't bite or scratch, ever. She knows we love her. At least *most* of us do." Charlotte glared at Daddy. "I'll bet she'll even go to sleep on your lap, Tessa. Here. Take her."

Charlotte picked up the cat and lowered her onto Tessa's lap. Tessa sucked in her breath and pressed her back into the bench. But the cat nestled down and wrapped her tail around herself again.

"Her's sleeping on me," Tessa said, looking pleased. She began to pet the cat's fur shyly, as if she still weren't quite sure how she felt about touching cats.

"Oh, isn't that cute?" said Mom. "See, Tessa, the kitty won't hurt you. Kitties *are* nice."

"Nice kitty," said Tessa, still petting the cat's fur. The cat half opened her eyes and looked dreamily at Tessa. "Her's watching me."

"She's a nice cat," said Mom. She patted Tessa's hand and then turned to her book.

"Well." Daddy jumped up from his chair. "If I don't get the water boiling for those lobsters, we'll never eat tonight."

"I'll be down in a little while," said Mom. She took a sip of her lemonade and started reading.

Charlotte watched the deck door as the wind slammed it after Daddy. She took a deep breath and turned to Mom.

"Tessa and I have decided something," she said.

"Oh," Mom said, still reading. "What's that?"

"It's about the cat." Charlotte paused, then said in a rush, "If she doesn't belong to anyone else, we want to bring her back to New Jersey with us."

Mom looked up. "Charlotte, you know how Daddy feels about another cat."

"But you love the little yellow cat. Don't you, Mom? And I do and Tessa does."

"She's very sweet, Charlotte," Mom said. "But we already have a cat at home."

"Howard's *your* cat," Charlotte said. Tessa nodded.

"That's not true," Mom said. "Howard's everyone's cat. It's just that we aren't all Howard's people."

"Howard bite me," Tessa said.

"Only once," Mom reminded her. "And that was a long time ago."

"Howard only bit her once because she never went near him after that," Charlotte said.

"Tessa's a smart girl," Mom said. "What's more, Charlotte, we don't know if this cat's really a stray."

"But no one takes care of her," said Charlotte.

"I know it looks that way," said Mom.

"But we should make sure before we bring this up with Daddy."

"No one even feeds her," said Charlotte. "She was starving before we got here."

"Her owners may be neglectful and still exist," said Mom. "The people who live in that gray house down the hill might know something about the cat." She pointed over the hedge. "There are never any bathing suits on their clothesline, so they must live here year-round. Summer people would be swimming every day."

Mom snapped her book shut and stood up.

"Are you going to talk to them *now*?" Charlotte asked, feeling a little scared. She wanted to know about the cat and she didn't want to know, all at the same time. What if it was their cat, or belonged to someone they knew?

"Right now, I've got to help Daddy get dinner on the table," said Mom before she went in. "Maybe sometime tomorrow, Charlotte."

Charlotte crossed her fingers and held them up to Tessa. "Well," she said, "she didn't actually say no, did she?"

5

Daddy's Decision

Charlotte lay on her back on the old picnic table behind the summer house, with her fingers laced together beneath her head. She stared up at the raspberry sherbet–colored sky, listening hard to the sounds coming out through the open kitchen window. She could hear Mom's and Daddy's voices amid the clatter of getting dinner ready, but she couldn't tell what they were saying.

Were they talking about the cat?

A whole day had passed, and Mom still hadn't gone to the gray-house neighbors. She hadn't even mentioned it, and Charlotte hadn't wanted to ask in front of Daddy.

All afternoon at the beach, Charlotte had watched Daddy with an awful wiggly feeling in her stomach, hoping for a clue. Did he know what she'd told Mom about the cat?

Tessa took beach stones out of her plastic bucket, one by one, and set them out in a long line on the picnic bench. She began to hum.

"Shhh!" said Charlotte. "I can't hear."

Just then, the back screen door opened, and Mom stepped into the yard.

"I'm going to run down to the neighbors in that gray house, now, Charlotte," she said. "To see if they can tell me anything about the cat."

Charlotte sat up. "Does Daddy know?" she asked.

"Only that I'm going to the neighbors," said Mom. "Don't get your hopes up, Charlotte. The cat may belong to someone."

"She doesn't," said Charlotte.

"We'll see," said Mom, and she walked off.

"She's going, Tessa," Charlotte whispered. "She's going to ask the neighbors about our cat." She crossed her fingers and held them up.

Tessa crossed her fingers, too. She showed Charlotte. "See? Two."

"Good," said Charlotte. "Remember how this worked before when the little cat first came? Well, if we keep them crossed till Mom gets back, the cat will be ours to keep."

"Her is coming home with us?" Tessa asked.

"Oh, I don't know. I don't know," Charlotte said. "But, I want her to, so much."

Charlotte shivered. Suddenly, she felt cold and her fingers ached. She had to go to the bathroom, but she wanted to stay outside where she could watch for Mom. She crossed her legs.

"It's double luck if you cross your legs too, Tessa," she said.

Tessa crossed her legs.

"Bubble up," she giggled.

"*Double luck*, Tessa. I said *double luck*. Good grief," Charlotte said.

"Mommy!" shouted Tessa as Mom came through the opening in the hedge.

"C'mon, Tessa!" Charlotte untangled her legs and hopped off the table. Oh, please don't let her be anybody else's cat, she prayed as she raced across the grass.

"What did they say? What did they say?" Charlotte asked, running up to Mom.

"Come inside," Mom said. "Then Daddy can hear, too."

"So, what's with the neighbors?" Daddy asked as they came into the kitchen. He stopped slicing tomatoes and leaned against the counter.

"Say it loud so I can hear you from the bathroom," Charlotte yelled, racing off.

Almost shouting, Mom began, "The neighbors said that the cat showed up late in the spring when the owners of this house were here getting things ready for the summer.

They said she didn't seem to belong to them, but the owners fed her while they were here. And she's been hanging around ever since."

"I guess she's been lucky that the summer renters have been feeding her," Daddy said as Charlotte came out.

"From the looks of her, not everyone has," Mom said.

"Well, she hasn't starved, anyway," said Daddy.

"See?" said Charlotte. "I knew she wasn't anybody's cat."

"My cat," said Tessa.

Charlotte rolled her eyes.

"To tell the truth," Mom said, "the neighbors didn't act particularly interested. They didn't seem like animal lovers to me."

"That settles it," said Charlotte. "She's coming home with us."

"Absolutely not!" said Daddy. "We've got a cat already. And we don't need another animal in the house." Daddy turned to Mom. "I told you we were going to get into this. Didn't I?"

"This isn't *another animal*," said Charlotte. "This is our own little cat that we love."

"Two cats?" Daddy said. "We'd be up to our necks in cat fur and spend half our lives vacuuming."

"I can vacuum," Charlotte said.

"My turn," said Tessa. "I do it."

"And this cat has very short fur that stays right there on her body," said Charlotte.

"And what about Howard?" asked Daddy. "It doesn't seem fair to show up with a new cat after we've been gone for a week. He's been our only cat for a long time. And he's getting to be an old man now."

"Oh, Howard will love this little cat. Won't he, Mom?" Charlotte asked.

"It's hard to know what Howard is going to like," Mom said.

"The cat's not even well," Daddy said. "She's half starved and infested with fleas. Have you seen the way she's always scratching at her ears? That's ear mites. And do you know what that means? Vet bills! Twice the cat fur! Twice the vet bills! The answer is definitely *no*."

"I still have eight dollars of my birthday money left," said Charlotte.

"It's Charlotte's birthday?" Tessa asked.

"Eight dollars! That will barely pay for the flea shampoo," Daddy shouted. "Charlotte, enjoy the cat while we're here, and when we go, we'll leave a big bag of Meow Mix with a note encouraging the next renters to do the same. End of discussion."

"That's a terrible idea!" Charlotte yelled, tears pricking at her eyes. "I want this cat, Tessa wants this cat and Mom wants this cat. You're the only one who doesn't. I don't think you even *like* cats at all."

"Are you ladies ganging up on me?" Daddy asked, looking at Mom.

"She is a very sweet little cat," said Mom.

"You are," Daddy said. "I can see that. Now if you'll excuse me, I'm going to get the hamburgers on the grill before the fire goes out."

He went out the back door, carrying the plate of hamburger patties.

"And what if the next people don't like cats?" Charlotte asked. "Then what?" She pushed past Tessa and ran upstairs before Mom could answer.

6

On the Deck

Charlotte had shut the door to her room, but she could hear Mom and Tessa come up the stairs and stop outside.

"Charlotte's crying," said Tessa from the other side of the door.

"Charlotte, are you coming down for dinner?" Mom asked.

"I'm not coming," Charlotte sobbed, but the words were all muffled in her pillow.

"We'd love to have you with us," said Mom.

Charlotte didn't answer her.

"It's Hamburger Specials, your favorite," Mom called through the door. Then Charlotte heard them go back downstairs.

When Charlotte finally came down, dinner was almost over. She silently piled a lettuce leaf and a slice of tomato onto her hamburger and smeared the inside of the roll with ketchup. Her face felt hot from crying, but her tears had finally stopped.

"Hi, Charlotte," Tessa said shyly.

"Yes. Welcome back," said Mom.

Charlotte looked down and said nothing.

They all kept eating.

Suddenly Daddy said too loudly, "Terrific hamburgers!"

"Mmmm," said Mom. "Good summer tomatoes."

Charlotte sniffed. She looked up and saw Tessa watching her with a scared-looking face. Then she stared back down at her plate.

"What do you say we have dessert up on the deck tonight?" asked Daddy. "The sunset should be spectacular after the weather we've had today."

"It was an awful day," Charlotte mumbled. She didn't look at Daddy.

"I want ice cream for dessert," Tessa said, brightening.

"Ice cream it is!" Daddy said, scraping his chair back from the table. "And two coffees, right?" he asked, looking at Mom.

She nodded, still chewing her last bite of hamburger.

"I don't want any more," said Charlotte. She pushed her plate away.

"All done," Tessa said, sliding her plate back, too.

"You're saving room for ice cream, right?" Daddy called from the kitchen.

"Ice cream!" said Tessa.

Charlotte didn't say anything. She carried her plate and glass to the sink. "C'mon, Tessa," she said quietly. "Let's go up."

When they were out on the deck, Charlotte plopped down on the bench.

"Oh, Tessa," she said. "Do you think Daddy will ever change his mind about the little yellow cat?"

"Ice cream coming on through!" Daddy shouted from behind the deck door.

Charlotte stared out at the far-off harbor. From the corner of her eye, she saw Daddy come out carrying a big red tray. With his bare foot, he kicked the door shut behind him.

"Ice cream!" shouted Tessa.

"Here you go," Daddy said, handing Tessa her dish. "Charlotte?" he asked, holding a dish of ice cream out to her.

"I don't want any," she grumbled.

"But you love chocolate chip," said Daddy.

"I said I didn't want any." Charlotte felt like she was about to cry again.

Daddy shrugged. "I guess I'll just have to have seconds then."

Tessa already had a ring of melted ice cream around her mouth.

How disgusting, thought Charlotte. Tessa doesn't even care about the cat. I hate you, Tessa.

The deck door opened and Mom came out. She sat down on the bench, next to Charlotte.

"No ice cream for you, Charlotte?"

"You all just go on eating ice cream like you don't even care!"

"Of course we care," Mom said. She tried to put an arm around her but Charlotte shrugged it away. "But Daddy is entitled to his feelings about this, too. And there would be problems and expenses. I'm sure the cat hasn't even had her shots."

"So we're just going to leave her here to die." Charlotte was sobbing again. She turned to Mom. "I can't believe you're on *his* side."

"C'mon, Charlotte," said Daddy. "The cat will be fine. She's made it this long, hasn't she? You heard what the neighbors said. She's been around since last April. She's a proven survivor."

"But you said she's got fleas and ear mites," said Charlotte. "And no one was even feeding her before we got here. She's going to get some terrible sickness without her shots."

"OK," said Daddy. "OK. We'll get her to a vet before we leave and get her the shots. I'll even give her a flea bath. Does that get me out of my bad guy role?"

"What a great idea!" said Mom. "And I'll buy her a flea collar." She turned to Charlotte. "Isn't it a great idea, Charlotte?"

"If we're going to do all these wonderful things for her, why can't we take her home with us?" Charlotte asked.

"Because *I* said we can't," Daddy said, collecting the ice-cream dishes on the tray. "That's why." Then he stamped back inside with the dishes all clinking against each other.

"I'll bet Emily's father would say OK," Charlotte shouted after him.

"I hope I can find a vet on Saturday," said Mom, checking her watch. "It's too late now to call, and we'll be leaving first thing Sunday morning."

"What difference does it make?" said Charlotte. "All the shots in the world aren't going to help if there's no one here to feed her."

"Under the circumstances, it's the best we can do," Mom said. She patted Charlotte's shoulder and stood up to go back inside.

"It's the best we can do," Charlotte repeated in a singsong voice when Mom was gone. "Sure it is. First Daddy and now Mom. I still can't believe that she's on his side."

With a soft *pumpf*, the cat jumped from the shower-stall roof and landed on the bench. Tessa pulled the cat onto her lap.

"See, I do it," she said, petting her over and over with both hands.

"Tessa, do you know there's only two days left till we have to go home? Really only one whole day and two nights, counting tonight. And then we'll never see this cat again." Charlotte began to cry quietly. That awful wiggly feeling was back in her stomach. She leaned over to bury her face in the cat's fur. The cat lifted its head and looked back at Charlotte.

"Poor Charlotte," Tessa said, patting her sister's head.

"Poor *little cat*. She's the one who'll be left all alone." Charlotte hunched over the cat, wetting the fur beneath her cheek with tears. Then she sat up and mopped her eyes with the backs of her hands.

"But she doesn't *have* to be alone," she said. "Not as long as we're still here, anyway. I just had a terrific idea, Tessa. A really terrific idea."

"What?" Tessa asked, smoothing down the cat's patch of spiky, wet fur.

"You'll see," said Charlotte.

"Girls!" Mom called to them from inside. "It's time to come in now."

"It's getting dark time," Tessa said, looking all around her.

"Yeah, let's go in." Charlotte lifted the cat from Tessa's lap and set her down on the bench. "Now, you stay right here, little cat. I'll be back."

But the cat jumped back up to the shower-stall roof and was on her way down to the ground before Charlotte had even opened the deck door.

From the threshold, Tessa called out.

"Goo-nye, little cat."

"Don't go far," Charlotte cried. "I'll be back."

· 7 ·

Charlotte's Idea

"I'm going to keep the cat with me every minute till we have to go," Charlotte announced loudly as she and Tessa came down the stairs. "You say she's not allowed in the house? Then I'm staying outside with her on the deck. All night, tonight and tomorrow night. I won't leave her alone for even one second, no matter what you say."

"Let's get something straight, Charlotte," said Daddy. "The no animals rule is the summer house owner's rule, not mine. Stop making me out to be such a complete ogre."

"No. You're not a *complete ogre*," said Charlotte. "You just want to leave a beautiful little cat all alone to die. That's all. Emily's father doesn't even leave Max when he goes on vacation."

"Are we back on that guy again?" asked Daddy.

"He's a lot nicer than you are," said Charlotte.

"That's enough," said Mom. "And you *cannot* sleep on the deck, Charlotte."

"I sleeping on a deck, too," said Tessa.

"I'm not going to sleep," said Charlotte. "I'm going to stay awake all night with my cat."

"Charlotte, that's a crazy idea. It's windy outside at night. And cold," said Mom.

"So? I'll bring the quilt from my bed," said Charlotte.

"Let her go," said Daddy quietly. "Let her go."

"All right," said Mom. "But Tessa, I want you in your own bed."

"OK," said Tessa in a small voice.

She never wanted to do it anyway, thought

Charlotte. Good. I want it to be just me and my cat. No three-year-old babies.

Charlotte went up to her room. She stomped around getting ready, yanking open dresser drawers and slamming them shut again. She pulled her old Conwell School sweat shirt on over her summer nightgown and wrapped the quilt from her bed around her pillow. It was a cool night, but she felt all sweaty.

Mom came in carrying Tessa. She dumped her on the bed, and they both settled back against the pillows for Tessa's bedtime story. Mom began to read, raising her voice above all of Charlotte's racket.

"You probably don't care," Charlotte said, interrupting her, "but Tessa held the cat all by herself. Didn't you, Tessa?"

"Her sleeps right here on *me*," Tessa bragged, patting her tummy.

"You had the kitty on your lap, Tessa? How nice," said Mom. "And you weren't scared?"

Tessa shook her head, smiling.

"Why should she be?" asked Charlotte. *"This* cat doesn't bite or scratch like *some* cats I could name!"

"Enough," said Mom. "Didn't I already say enough?"

"Don't worry," said Charlotte, "I'm going now anyway."

"No good-night kiss?" Mom asked.

"I'm not going to sleep, remember?" Charlotte asked.

"I remember," said Mom. "But I want one anyway."

"Me too," said Tessa.

Charlotte rolled her eyes and sighed, but she leaned over her pillow and quilt bundle to kiss Mom and Tessa.

"Daddy and I will be reading in the living room if you want anything," Mom said.

"Why should I?" Charlotte asked.

She had a hard time carrying everything. The quilt kept slipping down around her knees. And the pillow was so big she had to

keep both arms around it with her fingers
locked together to hang on.

When she got to the deck door, Daddy
was standing there looking out.

"I don't see the cat, Charlotte," he said.

"She's out there," said Charlotte, hoping
that she was. She tried to hook a finger
around the door latch without dropping everything.

"I'll get that for you," said Daddy, pushing the door open. "And remember, you can
come back in whenever you want."

"I won't want to," Charlotte said as the
screen door banged behind her.

Once she was out on the deck, Charlotte didn't feel as brave as she had inside. The deck was bright enough, with the house lights shining through the windows, but everything else was dark.

She hugged her pillow and quilt together and walked slowly to the edge of the deck.

When she looked down at the yard, she couldn't even see the old stone wall at the bottom of the hill.

"Kitty, kitty, kitty," she called softly. "Are you out there, little cat?" Nothing moved.

A little more loudly, she called, "Kitty, kitty, kitty."

Charlotte listened hard, looking out into the blackness. She didn't hear anything but the wind until . . . *Meow,* the cat was there, rubbing the side of her whiskery face against Charlotte's bare foot.

"You're here!" Charlotte cried. She dropped her bundle and hugged the cat. "I'm going to stay here with you all night."

The cat watched as Charlotte smoothed

the quilt out and stood her pillow up against the wall of the house. Then she sat down and pulled the cat into her lap. The cat pointed her nose in the air as Charlotte gently scratched under her chin. Her purr sounded like a tiny motor running.

"You poor thing," said Charlotte. "You don't have a family and nobody wants you. Just like Little Orphan Annie in the story. You don't even have a name."

The cat kept purring.

"I know what I'll call you. Little Orphan Annie." Charlotte tried it out. "Annie. I like it. But it's not true that nobody wants you. I want you and Tessa wants you, and I know, no matter what she says, that deep inside Mom wants you, too."

Charlotte pulled up the quilt, but it didn't quite cover them. She leaned over and laid her cheek against Annie's back.

"Oh, Annie, Annie, how could Daddy be so mean? How could he want to leave you here all alone?"

8

Little Orphan Annie

The room was very bright when Charlotte opened her eyes. She was upstairs in her summer house bed, and Tessa's bed was empty.

They must have brought her back inside last night and she'd slept late.

She ran downstairs, but there was no one in the kitchen. The house was quiet.

"Is that you, Charlotte?" Daddy called. "I'm out here on the porch."

She stood still.

Where was Tessa? Where was Mom? She didn't want to talk to Daddy. Especially alone.

She slowly pushed the screen door open and stepped out onto the porch.

Daddy was sitting in the faded yellow director's chair, with his book open on his lap. Near Daddy's feet, Annie was eating Meow Mix from the metal bowl. Tessa must have fed her. The cat looked up at Charlotte, then went right back to eating.

"You brought me in, and I didn't want you to," said Charlotte.

"Yeah, well," said Daddy, "it got pretty cold out here last night."

"I was OK," said Charlotte. "Where are Mom and Tessa?"

"They're at the vet," Daddy said. "Actually, it's the vet's son. The real vet doesn't get here till August, so we can't get the shots. But, he's got the good kind of flea shampoo like we had for Howard, and he thinks he can find some ear mite stuff."

"So what?" said Charlotte. "With no one to take care of her, Annie's probably going to die anyway."

"Annie?" Daddy said.

"I named her Annie," said Charlotte. "You know, like Little Orphan Annie in the story—*the one that nobody wants*."

"Little Orphan Annie, huh?" said Daddy.

"Well, just Annie for short," said Charlotte.

"But I thought *you* wanted her," said Daddy.

"*And* Mom. *And* Tessa." Charlotte felt her face getting hot.

"Looks like I'm outvoted, then," said Daddy.

"What?"

"I said it looks like I'd better go along with the crowd," said Daddy.

"What do you mean?" asked Charlotte.

"I mean," said Daddy, "if you still want to, you can bring Annie home with you."

"I can? I can? Oh, Daddy, thank you! Thank you! Thank you!"

Charlotte's head thunked against Daddy's chest as she flung herself at him. She squeezed him till she felt her arms would snap.

"You're even nicer than Emily's dad," she said.

"That's quite a compliment," Daddy said. "But Mom's the one to thank. She talked me into it."

"Oh, you'll love having this cat live with us, Daddy," Charlotte said.

"I guess I'm going to find that out. Aren't I?" Daddy said.

Charlotte let go of Daddy and picked up Annie. She held her up in the air over her face, with her legs dangling down. Annie didn't seem to mind having her breakfast interrupted.

"You're coming with us, Annie," she said, hugging the cat. "You're going to live in New Jersey!" Then Annie wriggled out of Charlotte's arms and climbed up onto her shoulder. Charlotte arranged Annie around the back of her neck like a fuzzy collar.

"I know that Howard's going to like Annie, too," Charlotte said, reaching up to smooth Annie's fur. "They'll probably be best friends."

"I don't know about that, Charlotte," said Daddy. "I'm hoping that Howard doesn't realize she's there. He *is* a little on the dumb side, which in this case could be in our favor."

"They're here!" Charlotte shouted as the car came up the driveway. She held up the cat. "Tessa! Tessa!" she screamed. "We can keep the cat. Daddy says we can take Annie home!"

"Annie?" said Tessa.

"Here, you hold her."

Tessa clutched Annie against her with both arms.

"I named her Little Orphan Annie, and we're going to take her home with us," said Charlotte. "Daddy said."

"I taking Little Awful Annie home," said Tessa.

"*Orphan*, Tessa. The word is *orphan*. Oh, just call her Annie, OK? She's not an orphan anymore, anyway."

"My Annie," said Tessa. She swayed back and forth, holding the cat to her chest.

"Annie," said Mom. "I like it, Charlotte. It's a wonderful name for her."

"Thanks, Mom," said Charlotte, putting her arms around Mom's waist. "I mean for talking to Daddy and everything."

"He was a pushover," said Mom in a loud whisper.

"I don't know about that," said Daddy. "But it has been said that I'm as nice as Emily's dad."

"Nicer," said Charlotte.

Charlotte let go of Mom.

"Did you get Annie's stuff?" she asked.

"Flea shampoo, ear mite medicine and a special box to bring her home in," said Mom.

She went to the car and pulled out a red and white cardboard box. The box had a handle on top and holes punched in its sides to let the fresh air in.

"Now, how about if you put the box in the house and help me get the fleas off this new cat of ours?" said Mom. "It's our last beach day, and I don't intend to waste it standing around here."

Charlotte ran inside with the cat box. "We can use that dishpan under the sink," she said.

"I get it," said Tessa, pushing past.

Daddy held Annie still on the grass while Mom scooped warm water over her from the plastic dishpan. She struggled to get away, but Daddy knew how to hold her tight without hurting her.

"Wow! She's really skinny now," Charlotte said, as Mom lathered her up with the flea shampoo.

"Don't you worry," Mom said to the cat in a soft voice. "We're almost done. We're almost done."

Tessa and Charlotte poured measuring cups of water over Annie to rinse the shampoo bubbles off.

"Watch out for her eyes," Daddy said as they poured.

Annie stopped trying to get away, but she still didn't look very happy.

"I think you've got all the shampoo off, now," Mom said. "All finished, little cat."

Charlotte tried to wrap an old towel around Annie, but as soon as Daddy let her go, she ran off.

She stopped a little way away from them

to shake the water from her front paws. Then she ran through the opening in the hedge.

Charlotte went after her, calling, "Kitty, kitty, kitty! Annie, come back here!" But when she looked down the hill, the cat was just disappearing around the corner of the gray house.

"She hated that bath!" Charlotte said. "I hope she doesn't run away now."

"Don't worry, she'll be back for dinner," Daddy said. "By the time we're home from the beach this afternoon, she'll be all dry and fluffy."

"And without fleas," said Mom.

"Goo-bye, Little Awful Annie," Tessa called after the cat.

"Now get your things ready for the beach," said Mom. "And let's get going."

"The car leaves in five minutes," said Daddy.

At the beach, the waves chased Charlotte and Tessa up onto the sand. They screamed

over their shoulders as they ran away from
the water that lapped at their heels. But it
was a laughing kind of screaming.

Later, Daddy took them on a long walk
down the beach while Mom napped on the
blanket. Tessa had to take little running
steps to keep up with Daddy and Charlotte.

Daddy pointed to a ferry on its way out
from the harbor.

"That's where we'll all be tomorrow," he
said. "Heading home."

Waves came in to splash against their ankles as they walked. Then the water went

back out again, leaving tiny holes in the wet sand, as if it had been poked with a pencil point.

They kept walking till they got to the place where it was too rocky to go any farther.

On the way back, they collected almost a whole bucketful of shells and rocks to bring home to New Jersey. The bucket got so heavy that Daddy had to carry it for them.

"I was about to send out a rescue party," Mom said when she saw them.

"Pretty rocks!" Tessa held one up for Mom to see.

Everyone else on the beach seemed to be going home but them.

"I want to go back to the house now," said Charlotte.

"Don't rush," said Daddy. "This is it till next year, Charlotte."

At last Daddy began folding up the beach chairs. He and Mom each grabbed an end of the blanket and snapped it in the air between them, scattering sand all over the place.

Then they carried their gear back to the car for the last time. Charlotte tied one of Mom's bandanas to her folded-up beach chair and dragged it behind her like a sled.

"Goo-bye, ocean." Tessa waved as she climbed into the backseat.

"See you next year," said Mom.

Charlotte took a deep breath before she got into the car. She wanted to bring the smell of the ocean back home with her.

"I can't believe that our vacation's almost over," Daddy said, driving back.

"The last beach day is always a little sad," said Mom.

"I say goo-bye, ocean," said Tessa.

They picked up their last vacation lobsters at the fish market and drove through the village to say good-bye. It was a long, slow ride back to the summer house. Finally, Daddy turned up the driveway.

Annie was waiting by the porch steps. She ran up to the car as it stopped, just as she had on that very first day.

Charlotte cuddled Annie in her arms.

"Her's fluffy," said Tessa, reaching up to touch the cat.

"I guess she forgave us for that bath. Or maybe she forgot by now." Charlotte pushed her face into Annie's fur. "Mmmm. You smell so good!" she said.

"She looks terrific," Mom said to Daddy. "Doesn't she look terrific?"

"She looks terrific. She looks terrific," said Daddy. "I'm already sold on this cat, remember?"

After dinner, they sat up on the deck for the last time, to watch the sailboats come in.

"When we come back next year," Charlotte said, "Nora will have two cats to take care of."

"And no matter what shows up, we're not taking it home," said Daddy. "NO MORE ANIMALS!" He said it in an angry-sounding voice, but his hand kept stroking Annie, who was curled up on his lap.

"I'll put my blue doll blanket in the bottom of the box to make a bed for you, Annie," Charlotte said. "It'll be all nice and soft." She scratched around the cat's ears. It looked to Charlotte like Annie was almost smiling.

"I'll be calling you early tomorrow morning," Mom reminded them. "We're on the ten o'clock ferry, and we've still got packing to do."

"You're coming home with us," Charlotte whispered in the cat's ear. Annie opened her eyes and shook her head, as if the whisper tickled, or maybe it was her ear mites.

Charlotte lifted Annie up from Daddy's lap so she could look. "Say good-bye to the sailboats," she said.

"Goo-bye, sailboat," Tessa said, waving.

"Not you, Tessa." Charlotte sighed, putting the cat down on the bench. "Let's go to bed before you drive me completely crazy."

· 9 ·

Going Home

Mom called them early the next morning.

"C'mon, you sleepyheads!" she shouted. "Get up and get packing."

"We have to feed Annie first," Charlotte said, hopping out of bed.

"*My* turn," said Tessa.

"Hurry back in here then," Mom said. "The ferry leaves at ten o'clock."

They almost tripped over each other as the screen door swung open.

Annie wasn't on the porch.

"It's early," Charlotte said. "She doesn't expect us so early, Tessa." But still, they yelled, "Annie!"

Charlotte ran down to the stone wall where the chipmunks lived, and Tessa ran after her.

"Kitty, kitty, kitty," they called.

The cat didn't come.

They went up around the edge of the yard, where the blackberries grew in tangles. Too prickly in there for a cat. But Charlotte stood on her tiptoes to look in the bushes anyway. "Are you in there, Annie?" she asked.

They ran around the back, near the clump of weeds where the rusty wagon was.

"*Ps-s-st*, Annie!"

Charlotte's mouth was all dry from calling. Her throat had begun to ache.

She ran to the opening in the hedge and looked down the hill.

"Annie, come here!" Charlotte screamed hoarsely.

Sheets and clothes flapped on the grayhouse clothesline. Annie wasn't down the hill, either.

"My feet hurt," whined Tessa. They had gone off without their shoes.

"You're such a baby, Tessa," Charlotte shouted at her. "Who cares about your stupid feet? Our cat's gone!"

Charlotte ran back to the house with Tessa behind her.

Charlotte had to gulp for air as she ran into the kitchen.

"She's gone," Charlotte cried. "Annie's gone."

"Her's not here," Tessa said, shrugging.

Mom stopped loading the cooler and smoothed back Charlotte's hair with her hand.

"Charlotte, honey, calm down," she said. "She'll turn up. The cat's been here every day for a week. She's not going to disappear now."

"But she has," said Charlotte. "She's gone."

"Mom's right," Daddy said. "Have some breakfast and get yourselves dressed. The cat will show up. I'm sure of it."

"I hungry," said Tessa.

Daddy poured Bran Chex and milk for both of them and sliced a banana on top, half for Charlotte and half for Tessa.

Charlotte took only a few bites, then pushed back her bowl.

"That's all I want," she said. "I'm not hungry."

"I not hungry, too," said Tessa.

Charlotte ran out to the porch again, and Tessa ran after her.

"Kitty, kitty, kitty," they called. "AN-NIE!"

Charlotte turned to Tessa. "She'll be here after we get dressed," she said. "Let's go in."

As they pulled on their shorts and T-shirts, Charlotte could hear Mom down in the yard calling.

"AN-NIEEE!"

Then Daddy's voice, much louder and deeper, "C'mon, cat!"

When they didn't call up to her, Charlotte knew that Annie hadn't come for them, either.

"We've still got nearly an hour," Charlotte heard Daddy say as they came back inside. "She'll be back."

"Keep packing," Mom shouted up the

stairs. "We've got to be out of here by nine thirty."

Charlotte and Tessa had to find all their books and cassette tapes and put them in the green basket that would ride with them on the long trip home. Charlotte knew they hadn't found them all yet, but she stopped anyway and ran outside again.

"Annie!" Charlotte's voice sounded very high. Her throat really ached now. The cat didn't come. Charlotte went back in.

"I don't understand this," Mom said, pushing the last towel into a big plastic trash bag. "Where would she go?"

Daddy called the ferryboat people to see if they could get on a later ferry. They couldn't. The ferries were all full, and they couldn't stay another day. Daddy and Mom both had to go back to work tomorrow, and new people were coming to stay at the summer house that afternoon.

"They'll get *our* cat," said Charlotte.

"Who got my cat?" asked Tessa.

"I know," said Charlotte. "I'll leave a note. We can come back to get her if the next visitors find her. Can't we, Mom?"

"Of course," said Mom.

"Now how will we do that?" Daddy asked.

"I'll take some time off work," said Mom quickly. "I don't know how we'll do it. We just will. That's all."

Charlotte found a pad and some paper and wrote:

Dear Next Visitor,

We can't find our cat, and we have to go home. She is small and yellow and sweet. Her name is Annie and I love her very much. If you find her, please call us in New Jersey and we will come back to get her. Our phone number is 201–555–6358.

Charlotte

It was almost nine thirty when they finished packing the car.

"Let's try once more, and then we really have to go," Daddy said. "We've got to check in by nine forty-five or we'll lose our reservation."

"This is just awful," said Mom. "I was sure she'd be back by now."

"Kitty, kitty, kitty," they called in their different voices, running all around the yard. "Annie!"

She didn't come.

"I hate to say it, but we've got to get going," Daddy said. "We're late already."

They walked slowly to the car. Charlotte walked backward, so she could keep looking. She was crying, but she kept pushing the tears back up into her eyes with the side of her finger, as if she could stop them that way. She carried the cat box in her other hand. It banged against her leg with an empty sound.

Daddy started the engine. "Maybe she just wanted to stay a summer house cat," he said.

Charlotte and Tessa and Mom rolled down their windows and kept calling all the way to the end of the driveway. The car was filled with a sad quiet as it bumped along the dirt road, away from the summer house. The only sound was Charlotte's sniffling.

They were just turning onto Beach Road when Charlotte put her hand in her pocket. "The note!" she screamed. "Look! I forgot to leave the note!"

The paper was folded over and over into a

tiny square. Charlotte didn't remember folding it up or even putting it in her pocket.

"Now we'll never get her back. I can't believe I'm so stupid!"

"Charlotte, you are *not* stupid," said Mom. "You're upset. It's easy to forget things when you're upset."

"We have to go back," Charlotte cried. "We have to."

"Charlotte, you know that's impossible," Daddy said.

"We're late already, honey," said Mom. "Look at the line of cars waiting for the ferry."

Dear Next Visitor,
We can't find our cat and we have to go home. She is small and yellow and sweet. Her name is Annie and I love her very much. If you fi___ ___ ___se call us in New Jersey and ___ ___ come back to get her. ___ ___ ___e number is 201-555-6358.

Charlotte

Daddy pulled in behind the last car and turned off the key.

"But what time is it?" asked Charlotte. "It would only take a minute to go back. Please? Please?"

"It's nine fifty. I've got to let them know we're here," Mom said, jumping out. "We'll call about the cat from home, Charlotte." And then she was gone.

"We don't have to stay in the car," said Daddy. "Let's get out and look at the boats while we're waiting." He handed two tissues back over his shoulder.

Getting the tissue made Charlotte cry even harder. "I really loved that little cat," she sobbed. "I can't believe I forgot the note."

"Sometimes animals do things that are hard for people to understand," said Daddy.

"I love my cat," said Tessa.

Tessa doesn't understand that Annie is really gone, thought Charlotte. What do three-year-olds know about anything?

They all got out. Charlotte and Daddy

leaned against the car and stared out at the water. Charlotte tried to make herself stop crying, but tears kept filling her eyes and running down her face all by themselves.

Tessa squatted down, pushing the gravel into little piles with the sides of her hands.

"Where did she go, Daddy?" Charlotte wasn't even trying to stop crying anymore.

"I wish I knew," Daddy said. "I only wish I knew, Charlotte."

Mom came up to them suddenly, out of breath. "The ferry's been delayed a half hour," she said. "I'm going back with the note."

"You'll never make it," Daddy said. "Are you crazy?"

"Probably," Mom said, sliding behind the wheel. "Quick, Charlotte. Give it to me."

"I'm coming with you," Charlotte cried, and jumped into the front seat with Mom before anyone could stop her.

"I coming, too!" cried Tessa.

"You wait here with me, Tessa," Daddy said, lifting her up onto his shoulders. "You'll be the scout."

"Don't let the ferry leave without us!" Mom hollered out the car window. Bits of gravel flew from under the wheels as they pulled out of the line of cars and drove off.

"Please, be there, Annie," Charlotte prayed softly. "Please, be there."

"If she wasn't there before, she's probably not there now, either," Mom said. "This is a real long shot, Charlotte."

"I know, I know," said Charlotte.

"And," said Mom, "we still have Howard at home, don't forget."

"Howard," groaned Charlotte.

"Then maybe we could think about a new kitten," said Mom. "We could check at the animal shelter when we get home."

"But we wouldn't *know* a new kitten," said Charlotte. "We could end up with *another* Howard. Or worse."

"Another Howard," said Mom. "That would be a problem. But let's think positively, Charlotte. At least we're leaving the note. If Annie's not there today, maybe she'll show up later and someone will call us."

"I want her *now*," said Charlotte. "Today. Not later."

"Sometimes we have to wait for what we want," said Mom. "Even when we want it very, very much."

Suddenly they were there.

Charlotte stared out the window at the porch. The two faded director's chairs and the two metal bowls were there where they had left them, but no cat.

"I'll put up the note while you have a last look around," Mom said, climbing out.

Charlotte got out and slammed her door.

She handed Mom the note without looking at her, already searching the yard with her eyes. For a minute, she stood perfectly still, just looking very hard. Then she ran down the hill shouting, "KITTY! KITTY! ANNIE!"

She ran back up and around the summer house, past the clothesline, and stopped just before she got to the opening in the hedge. She closed her eyes and crossed her fingers.

Please, Annie, please be there.

With her eyes still closed, she walked slowly to the opening and called as loudly as she could.

Then Charlotte opened her eyes just as the cat came around the corner of the gray house and ran up the hill toward her.

Charlotte raced to meet her and grabbed Annie up in a hug. The cat felt all soft and warm.

Then she ran back to the summer house with Annie in her arms, shouting, "Mom! I've got her! I've got Annie!"

"Oh, Charlotte," said Mom, coming out to the porch. "You found her."

"She found me," Charlotte said. "She came back."

"Thank goodness," Mom said, hugging both of them. "Now, pop her into the cat box while I pull down that note. We've got to get out of here. And, hurry. We're cutting it very close."

Mom slipped behind the wheel and Charlotte slid in next to her—with the cat. Mom drove leaning forward, as if she could get them there faster that way.

Annie kept meowing inside her box. She pushed her pink nose out through one of the

box's holes, and Charlotte stroked it with the crook of one finger.

"It's all right, Annie," she said. "We're going home. We're going home."

"I think we're just going to make it," Mom said, swerving the car into the parking lot.

The line of cars for the ferry almost reached the road. Mom had to park at the end, far from their old place in line.

Charlotte could see Daddy and Tessa still waiting down near the water. But they weren't looking at the boats. They were looking toward the road. Before Mom had even turned off the engine, Daddy was running to them, with Tessa bouncing on his shoulders.

Charlotte jumped out.

"I found Annie!" she yelled. But the wind seemed to blow her words away.

She pulled Annie's box out and held it up. And then she ran toward them, bumping the box with her knees, shouting, "It's Annie! I've got her. She's coming home."